Snow White

This book is dedicated to the first
Charles Santore in our family, my father.
—Charles Santore

STERLING and the distinctive Sterling logo are registered trademarks of
Sterling Publishing Co., Inc.

Library of Congress Cataloging-in-Publication Data

Snow White : a tale from the Brothers Grimm / illustrated by Charles
Santore.
p. cm.
Summary: Retells the tale of the beautiful princess whose lips were
red as blood, skin was white as snow, and hair was black as ebony.
ISBN 978-1-4027-7157-6
[1. Fairy tales. 2. Folklore--Germany.] I. Grimm, Jacob, 1785-1863.
II. Grimm, Wilhelm, 1786-1859. III. Santore, Charles, ill. IV. Snow
White and the seven dwarfs. English.
PZ8.S415575 2010
398.20943'02--dc22   2009040764m

Lot#:
2 4 6 8 10 9 7 5 3 1
03/10

Originally published in 1996 by Park Lane Press, a division of Random House Value Publishing, Inc.
This edition published in 2010 by Sterling Publishing Co., Inc.
387 Park Avenue South, New York, NY 10016
Illustrations © 1996 by Charles Santore
Distributed in Canada by Sterling Publishing
^{c}/o Canadian Manda Group, 165 Dufferin Street
Toronto, Ontario, Canada M6K 3H6
Distributed in the United Kingdom by GMC Distribution Services
Castle Place, 166 High Street, Lewes, East Sussex, England BN7 1XU
Distributed in Australia by Capricorn Link (Australia) Pty. Ltd.
P.O. Box 704, Windsor, NSW 2756, Australia

Sterling ISBN 978-1-4027-7157-6

For information about custom editions, special sales, premium and
corporate purchases, please contact Sterling Special Sales
Department at 800-805-5489 or specialsales@sterlingpublishing.com.

Designed by Chrissy Kwasnik.

Snow White

A TALE FROM THE
Brothers Grimm

❧

Illustrated by Charles Santore

♪ STERLING

New York / London

nce upon a time, in the middle of winter, when the snowflakes were falling like feathers on the earth, a queen sat at a window framed in black ebony, and sewed. And as she sewed and gazed out at the white landscape, she pricked her finger with the needle, and three drops of blood fell on the snow outside. The red droplets showed so clearly against the white snow that she thought to herself, *Oh, what wouldn't I give to have a child as white as snow, as red as blood, and as black as ebony!*

Soon after, her wish was granted, and a little daughter was born to her, with skin as white as snow, lips and cheeks as red as blood, and hair as black as ebony. They named her Snow White. But not long after the child's birth, the queen died.

After a year, the king married again. His new wife was a beautiful woman, but so proud and overbearing that she could not stand any rival to her beauty. She had a magic mirror, and when she stood before it gazing at her own reflection she would ask:

> *Mirror, Mirror, on the wall,*
> *Who is fairest of us all?"*

The mirror always replied:

> *"Queen, you are fairest*
> *of them all."*

Then she was happy, for she knew the mirror always spoke the truth.

But Snow White was growing prettier every day, and when she was seven years old she was as beautiful as the springtime, and fairer even than the queen herself.

One day when the queen asked her mirror the usual question, it replied:

"My Lady Queen, you are fair, 'tis true,
But Snow White is fairer far than you."

Then the queen flew into the most awful rage, and turned every shade of green in her jealousy. From that hour she hated poor Snow White, and every day her envy, hatred, and malice grew.

At last, she could endure Snow White's presence no longer, and, calling a huntsman to her, she said, "Take the child into the woods. You must kill her, and bring me proof that she is dead."

The huntsman had to obey his queen. He led Snow White out into the woods, but just as he was drawing out his knife to slay her, Snow White began to cry, and she said, "Oh, dear huntsman, spare my life, and I will promise to run into the wild forest and never return home again."

The huntsman paused for a moment. Then, because she was so young and sweet and pretty, he took pity on her, and said, "You are free to go, poor child." For he secretly thought that the wild beasts would soon eat her up. But his heart felt lighter, because he hadn't had to do the terrible deed himself. Then the hunter killed a young deer instead, and he brought the animal's heart to his queen as proof that he had carried out her evil command.

Now, when poor Snow White found herself alone in the big forest, she didn't know which way to turn, but she knew that she must run as far from the queen as she could go. There were so many strange noises in the forest—and the towering dark trees and their looming shadows looked fierce and ominous. She felt so frightened that she didn't know what to do, but she ran like the wind over sharp stones and through bramble bushes and across mountains. Sometimes the creatures of the wild darted right past her—bears and wolves and other beasts—but they did her no harm.

She ran as far as her legs would carry her, and as evening approached she saw a little house. Exhausted, she went inside to rest.

Everything was very small in the little house, but very clean and very neat. In the middle of the room there stood a little table, covered with a white tablecloth, and seven little plates and forks and spoons and knives and cups. Side by side against the wall there were seven little beds, all covered with quilts as white as snow.

Snow White felt so hungry and so thirsty that she ate a bit of bread and some food from each plate, and then drank a few drops from each cup.

$\mathcal{T}$hen, feeling tired and sleepy, she lay down on one of the beds, but it wasn't comfortable. So she tried all the others in turn, but one was too long, and another was too short, and it was only when she got to the seventh that she found a bed that was just right. So she lay down upon it and fell asleep.

When it got quite dark the owners of the little house returned. They were seven dwarfs who worked in the mines deep down in the heart of the mountain. They entered with their seven little lamps, and they soon saw that someone had been in the room.

The first dwarf said, "Who's been sitting in my chair?"

The second said, "Who's been eating my bread?"

The third said, "Who's been tasting my dinner?"

The fourth said, "Who's been eating off of my plate?"

The fifth said, "Who's been using my fork?"

The sixth said, "Who's been cutting with my knife?"

And the seventh said, "Who's been drinking out of my cup?"

Then the first dwarf looked around and saw a little hollow in his bed, and he asked, "Who's been lying on my bed?"

The others came running, and when they saw their beds, cried out, "Somebody has been lying on ours, too."

But when the seventh dwarf came to his bed, he jumped back in amazement, for there was Snow White fast asleep. So he called to the others, who came hurrying over. When they saw Snow White lying there, they gasped with surprise.

"Goodness gracious!" they cried. "What a beautiful child!"

They were so enchanted by her beauty that they did not wake her.

The seventh dwarf had to sleep with his companions one hour in each bed, in order to get through the night.

In the morning when Snow White saw the seven little dwarfs she felt very frightened. But they were so friendly and kind that she said, "Hello, I am Snow White."

Then she told them how her stepmother had ordered her put to death, and how the huntsman had spared her life, and how she had run the whole day long till she had come to their house.

The dwarfs, when they heard Snow White's sad story, asked her, "Will you stay and keep house for us, cook, do the washing, sew, and knit? We could share our home with you and be your friends."

"Yes," answered Snow White. "I will gladly do all you ask."

And so she lived with them. Every morning the dwarfs went into the mountain to dig for gold, and in the evening when they returned home, Snow White always had their supper ready for them. But during the day the girl was left all alone, so the good dwarfs warned her, saying, "Beware of your stepmother. She will soon find out that you are here, and whatever you do, don't let anyone into the house."

The queen, believing Snow White to be dead, asked her mirror:
   "Mirror, mirror, hanging there, Who in all the land's most fair?"
And the mirror replied:
   "My Lady Queen, you are fair, 'tis true,
      But Snow White is fairer far than you.
         Snow White, who dwells with the seven little men,
            Is as fair as you, as fair again."

   When the queen heard these words she was so horrified that she could not speak, for the mirror always spoke the truth, and she knew now that the huntsman must have deceived her—and Snow White was still alive. She pondered day and night how she might destroy Snow White, for as long as she felt she had a rival in the land, her jealous heart knew no rest.

   At last she hit upon a plan. She stained her face and dressed herself as an old peddler woman, so that she was quite unrecognizable. In this disguise she crossed seven mountains until she came to the house of the seven dwarfs.

When she arrived, she knocked at the door, calling out, "Pretty wares to sell!"

Snow White peeped out the window and said, "Good day. What do you have there?"

"Nice wares, pretty wares," answered the woman, "laces of every shade and description," and she held up one that was made of brightly colored silk.

Surely I can let the honest woman in, thought Snow White; so she unlocked the door and bought the prettiest lace.

"Good gracious, child!" said the old woman. "How beautiful you are! Come, I'll lace your dress up properly."

Snow White, suspecting no evil, agreed—but the old woman laced her so quickly and so tightly that it took Snow White's breath away, and she fell down dead.

"Now you are no longer the fairest," said the wicked old woman, and she hurried away.

In the evening the seven dwarfs came home. What a fright they got when they saw their dear Snow White lying on the floor, still and cold! They lifted her up tenderly, and when they saw how tightly laced her dress was, they cut the lacing, and she began to breathe and gradually came back to life.

When the dwarfs heard the whole story, they said, "You can be sure the old woman was none other than the queen. In the future you must be sure to let no one in if we are not here in the house with you."

As soon as the wicked queen got   home, she asked her mirror:
"*Mirror, mirror, hanging there, Who in all the land's most fair?*"
And the mirror answered as before:
"*My Lady Queen, you are fair, 'tis true,*
But Snow White is fairer far than you.
Snow White who dwells with the seven little men,
Is as fair as you, as fair again."
The queen became as pale as death when she realized that Snow White was still alive.

This time, she said to herself, *I will think of something that will put an end to her once and for all.*

Using her witchcraft, the queen made a poisonous comb. Then she put on a different disguise and again crossed the seven mountains. When she reached the house of the seven dwarfs she called out, "Pretty wares for sale!"

Snow White looked out the window. "You must go away, for I may not let anyone in," she said.

"But surely you are not forbidden to look out?" asked the old woman, and she held up the beautiful comb.

Snow White liked the comb so much that she forgot the dwarfs' warning and opened the door.

"Now let me comb your hair properly for you," said the old woman.

Poor Snow White again suspected no evil, but hardly had the comb touched her hair than the poison worked and she fell down unconscious.

The wicked woman cackled as she hurried away.

Fortunately, the seven dwarfs soon returned home. When they saw Snow White lying dead on the ground, they knew that her wicked stepmother had been back. They found the poisonous comb, and when they pulled it out of her hair, Snow White woke up and told her story.

"You must remember our warning," said the dwarfs. "Do not open the door to anyone!"

As soon as the queen got home she asked her mirror:
"*Mirror, mirror, hanging there,*
Who in all the land's most fair?"
And it replied as before:
"*My Lady Queen, you are fair, 'tis true,*
But Snow White is fairer far than you.
Snow White who dwells with the seven little men,
Is as fair as you, as fair again."
When the queen heard this she shook with fury.

"Snow White shall die," she cried. "Yes, though it cost me my own life."

Then she went to a secret chamber and prepared a poisonous apple. It looked beautiful and delicious, but anyone who took a bite would instantly die.

The apple was so cleverly made that only one half was poisonous. When it was ready, the queen disguised herself as a peasant and again crossed the seven mountains to the seven dwarfs' cottage. This time Snow White leaned her head out the window and called, "I may not let anyone in. The seven dwarfs have forbidden me to do so."

"Are you afraid of being poisoned?" asked the old woman with a sly smile. "See, I will cut this apple in half. I'll eat one half and you can eat the other."

Snow White longed to eat the tempting fruit, and when she saw the peasant woman eating some, she couldn't resist. But hardly had the first bite passed Snow White's lips than she fell down dead. Then the eyes of the cruel queen sparkled with glee, and she cried, "Aha! This time the dwarfs surely will not be able to bring you back to life!"

When she got home, the queen asked her mirror:

"Mirror, mirror, on the wall,
Who's the fairest of us all?"

And this time the mirror replied:

"Queen, you are the fairest of them all."

Then her jealous heart was at rest—at least as much at rest as a jealous heart can ever be.

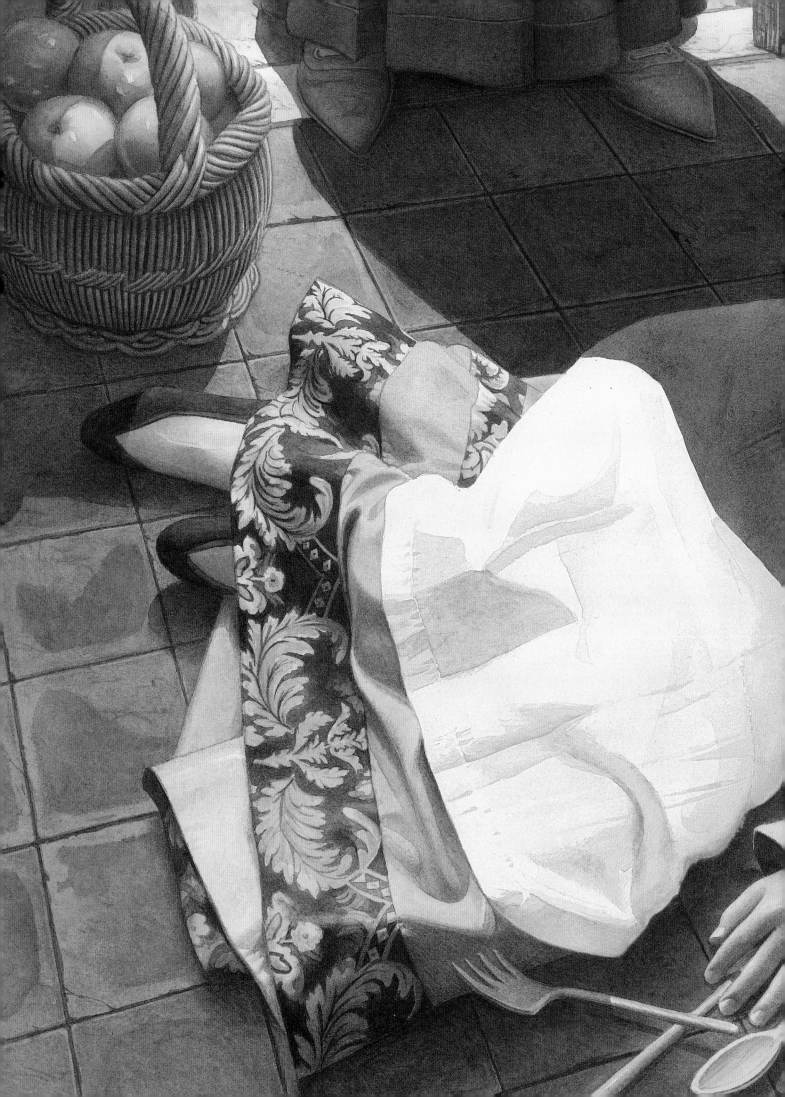

When the dwarfs returned home, they found Snow White lying on the ground and were afraid that this time she was truly dead. They lifted her up, and combed her hair, and washed her face. But all was in vain, for Snow White did not awaken. So they laid her down gently upon a long, flat stone, and all seven watched and mourned her for three whole days. Then it was time to bury her, but her cheeks were still rosy, and her face looked just as it did while she was alive, so they said, "We will never bury Snow White in the cold ground."

*I*nstead they
made a coffin of glass so they
could continue to look at her, and they wrote her name upon
it in golden letters.

They carried the coffin to the top of the mountain, and
from that day on, one of the dwarfs always sat by her side.
The birds of the air came, too, and cried for Snow White.
First came an owl, then a raven, and last came a dove.

And thus Snow White lay for many years, and still she looked as though she were only asleep— for always she was as white as snow, as red as blood, and as black as ebony.

One day a prince passing through the forest stopped at the dwarfs' house. Then he saw Snow White's glass coffin on the mountain and read her name in gold letters. He begged the dwarfs to let him take her away. But they said, "We will not part with her for all the gold in the world." At last, however, they took pity on him, for he seemed so distraught; and they told the prince he could take Snow White home to his palace.

But the moment his servants lifted up the coffin, they stumbled and nearly dropped it. The jolt made the piece of poisoned apple fall from between Snow White's lips, and she instantly awoke, and asked, "Where am I? Who are you?"

The prince just smiled with joy. Then he told her all that had happened, and said, "I promise to love you better than all the world. Come with me to my father's palace, and you shall be my wife."

Snow White consented, and went home with the prince; and everything was prepared with great pomp and splendor for their wedding.

Everyone in the whole land was invited to the feast, even Snow White's old enemy, the wicked queen. As she was dressing herself in fine rich clothes, the queen looked in the glass and said:

"Tell me, mirror, tell me true!
Of all the ladies in the land
Who is fairest? Tell me who?"
And the glass answered:
"Queen, thou art fairest here, I hold,
But the young queen is fairer, a thousandfold."

When the evil woman heard this, she shook with anger. But her envy and curiosity were so great that she could not help setting out to see the bride. And when she arrived, and saw that it was none other than Snow White, the queen was frozen with fright.

Then the wicked queen was commanded to put on a pair of magic slippers. The minute they were on her feet, the slippers forced her to dance and dance, faster and faster, until she dropped down dead.

There was great rejoicing in the hall, and Snow White and the prince lived in the palace and reigned happily over the land for many, many years.

THE END

About the Artist

Charles Santore has received numerous awards for artistic excellence, both for his past achievements in the magazine and advertising fields, and more recently for his illustrations for *The Wizard of Oz, Aesop's Fables,* and *The Little Mermaid.*

In 1992, he was honored for his work in book illustration with a major exhibition at the Brandywine River Museum. In addition, a selection of his paintings for *The Wizard of Oz* were used as the scenic backdrops for a major television performance of the work in 1995.

More recently, in 2009, Santore was chosen to create the official poster for the National Book Festival sponsored by The Library of Congress.

He lives and works in Philadelphia.